It'll Only Be STRONGER

written by:
Pamela Gaskin Huston

tate publishing
CHILDREN'S DIVISION

Published by Tate Publishing & Enterprises, LLC
127 E. Trade Center Terrace | Mustang, Oklahoma 73064 USA
1.888.361.9473 | www.tatepublishing.com

Tate Publishing is committed to excellence in the publishing industry. The company reflects the philosophy established by the founders, based on Psalm 68:11,
"The Lord gave the word and great was the company of those who published it."

Book design copyright © 2015 by Tate Publishing, LLC. All rights reserved.
Cover and interior design by Eileen Cueno
Illustrations by Lucent Ouano

Published in the United States of America

ISBN: 978-1-68142-695-2
1.Juvenile Fiction / Nature & The Natural World / General
2. Juvenile Fiction / Social Issues / Values & Virtues
15.06.24

This Book Belongs To:

_____

This book is dedicated to my dad,
Bobby "Gacky" Gaskin,
for being the strongest "tree" I'll ever
know.

One cool spring morning, the man came home with a seed. To everyone else, it was just a seed. It was nothing special to anyone but the man. The man saw potential in that little seed, believed in what it could grow to be, and he knew just what he needed to do. The man planted his newly found seed. He didn't use any special soil, only dirt. He didn't add extraordinary chemicals, just plain water every day. No one thought the seed would grow, but the man knew better, and so he said to the doubters, "It'll only be stronger..."

Through the spring rains, nothing seemed to happen. Everyone told the man the seed wasn't doing anything, but the man knew better, and so he said, "It'll only be stronger..."

The seed soon sprouted into a sad-looking seedling that everyone warned him would soon die. The man knew better, and so he said, "It'll only be stronger..."

Before long the summer sun was beating down on that sad little tree, but day after day the man visited the tree and gave it water. Everyone warned him that the tree would shrivel up and die, but the man knew better, and so he said, "It'll only be stronger..."

As fall came, the few leaves that the little tree had sprouted began to change colors and fell to the ground. Everyone felt certain this was the end of that little tree, but the man knew better, and so he said, "It'll only be stronger..."

Winter was harsh that year, and before long the little tree was surrounded by snow as deep as it was tall. Everyone shook their heads as the man cleared the snow away from the little tree, but the man knew it'll only be stronger...

As spring came, the little tree snapped back to life and sprouted many new leaves as it grew toward the sky. No one knew quite what to think, but the man knew, and so he said with a nod, "It'll only be stronger..."

In just a short while, the man had grandsons who loved the little tree almost as much as the man. They ran around the tree, jumped over the tree, and sometimes even ran into the little tree. Everyone thought for sure the little tree couldn't possibly survive this, but the man knew better, and so he said, "It'll only be stronger..."

Before long those grandkids were climbing the tree and hanging from its branches. Everyone still thought the tree couldn't possibly survive these rough boys and the little tree's days were surely numbered, but the man knew better, and so he said, "It'll only be stronger..."

As time went on, the little tree continued to grow to be big and strong. It provided homes to birds and squirrels and shade on hot days to everyone and the man. Everyone realized the man had been right to believe in the potential of that little seed.

Many years after that first early spring morning, the little tree still provides much pleasure to everyone, except no longer for the man.

It'll only be stronger...

About the Author

Pamela has been in the field of public education for twenty-one years as a teacher and is currently a principal at an elementary school in Moore, Oklahoma. Her father is "the man" in this story who never gave up on that seed and never gave up on her. Pamela strives to raise her two boys with the same conviction to always believe.

e|LIVE

listen|imagine|view|experience

AUDIO BOOK DOWNLOAD INCLUDED WITH THIS BOOK!

In your hands you hold a complete digital entertainment package. In addition to the paper version, you receive a free download of the audio version of this book. Simply use the code listed below when visiting our website. Once downloaded to your computer, you can listen to the book through your computer's speakers, burn it to an audio CD or save the file to your portable music device (such as Apple's popular iPod) and listen on the go!

How to get your free audio book digital download:

1. Visit www.tatepublishing.com and click on the e|LIVE logo on the home page.
2. Enter the following coupon code:
   5947-402a-f654-dffd-7d0e-214e-b308-6818
3. Download the audio book from your e|LIVE digital locker and begin enjoying your new digital entertainment package today!